ISBN 0-86163-652-X

Text and illustrations copyright ©1996 Sue Hall
This edition copyright ©1996 Award Publications Limited

First published 1996 by Award Publications Limited,
27 Longford Street, London NW1 3NS

Printed in Belgium

A Surprise for

Snatch

by **Sue Hall**

AWARD PUBLICATIONS LIMITED

Snatch and his friends gathered round to admire Smutty and Primrose's new home. They thought it looked wonderful, with the bright colours outside and a furry lining inside.

Smutty and Primrose couldn't wait to go to bed.

Although they liked their friends' new home, Horace and Boris preferred the large box that they slept in, especially as Boris was making a sign for it which said BEARS ONLY. That made it special!

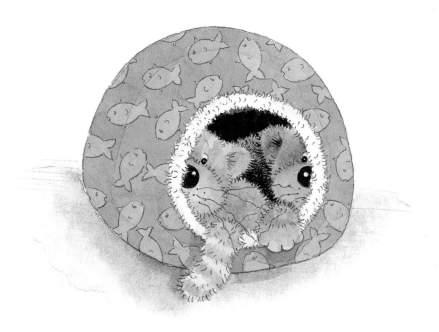

Spencer and Mark, the two mice, were just as proud of their home. In fact they thought that theirs was better because no one could see inside it. Behind the tiny hole in the wall was a cosy little bedroom, just for the two of them.

Even Gus the flying pig had his own special place. It was a beautiful blue velvet cushion with golden tassels on each corner and a label saying PRIVATE.

Snatch watched as Gus settled down for a rest on his cushion.

Snatch wandered up to the box belonging to the two bears. "Something like this would suit me," he thought. "I'll just see how it feels before Horace and Boris get back."

He climbed in and – oh dear! – he was stuck. What would the two bears say?

Snatch wriggled and pushed and pushed and wriggled, and after a lot of wriggling and pushing he managed to free himself from the box. But he hadn't seen the two bears behind the armchair, laughing at him trying to squeeze into their box.

Snatch looked at the goldfish swimming round in the bowl. "I'd better try and find a place of my own," he thought. "I know, I'll go and find my old basket. It's been a long time since I slept in there."

Then Snatch remembered why it had been such a long time – the basket was rather small for him. In fact he was bursting out of it in all directions, but it would have to do for now. Snatch wanted to go to sleep.

Boris saw Snatch trying to get into his basket and had an idea. He called the others together, all except for Gus who was fast asleep by now.

"Follow me," said Boris, and led them down the garden path to something almost hidden in the long grass.

"What is it?" asked Primrose.

Boris pulled away the grass until they could see a huge wooden box with a roof on top.

"It's a dog-house," Mark Mouse said excitedly.

"That's right," said Boris, "and we're going to make it nice for Snatch because everybody should have a place of their own to sleep in, like we do."

They all thought that this was a great idea. Soon they had cleared away all the grass and rubbish, and Boris painted a sign for the front which said HOME SWEET HOME.

It was finished.

"Quick!" yelled Mark Mouse. "Hide, everyone, Snatch is coming."

Peeping from behind the fence, they watched as Snatch stared in amazement.

"It's a kennel," Snatch muttered to himself. "It must be for me 'cos only dogs live in kennels and I'm the only dog here."

At that point the others jumped out from behind the fence. "We all helped to make it nice for you, Snatch," they chorused.

"It's the best kennel I've ever seen," Snatch said as he went inside. "Thank you all very much."

He settled down happily for a doze in his new home.

Snatch must have fallen fast asleep because the next thing he knew was that his friends were back with some of their things. They wanted to stay with him for the night, in case he felt lonely in his new home. Because it was a big kennel, there was enough room for all of them.

That night, as Snatch went to sleep, he thought how lucky he was to have such good friends to give him this lovely surprise.

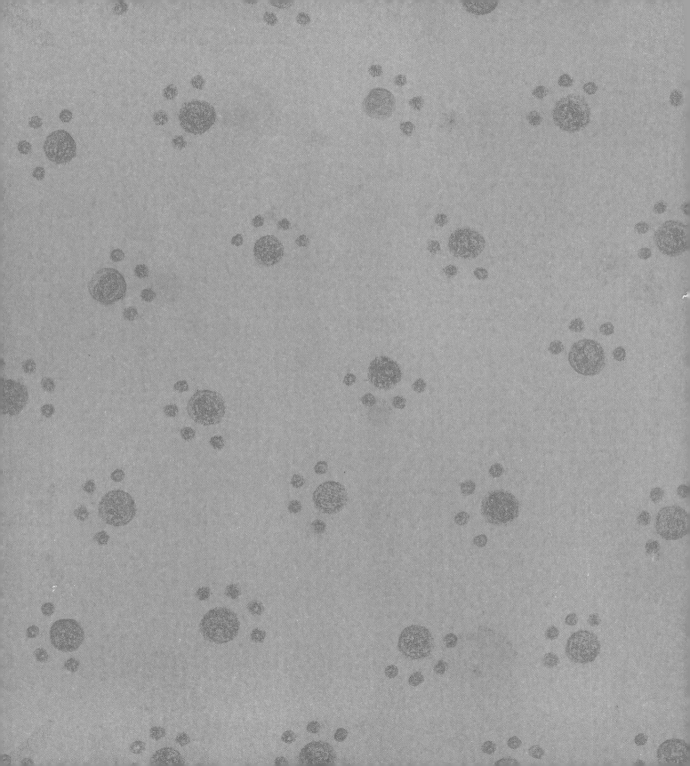